The Miracle Cures of Dr. Aira

The Miracle Cures of Dr. Aira

•

CÉSAR AIRA

Translated by Katherine Silver

A NEW DIRECTIONS PAPERBOOK ORIGINAL

Originally published by Ediciones Simurg, Buenos Aires, 1998; published in conjunction
   with the literary Agency Michael Gaeb/Berlin

Manufactured in the United States of America
New Directions Books are printed on acid-free paper.
First published as a New Directions Paperbook Original (NDP1238) in 2012
Published simultaneously in Canada by Penguin Books Canada Limited
Design by Erik Rieselbach

Library of Congress Cataloging-in-Publication Data
Aira, César, 1949–
[Curas milagrosas del Doctor Aira. English]
The Miracle Cures of Dr. Aira / by César Aira ; translated by Katherine Silver.
p. cm.
ISBN 978-0-8112-1999-0 (acid-free paper)
I. Silver, Katherine. II. Title.
PQ7798.1.I7C8713 2012
863'.64—dc23

2012012936

10 9 8 7 6 5 4 3 2 1

New Directions Books are published for James Laughlin
by New Directions Publishing Corporation
80 Eighth Avenue, New York, NY 10011

THE MIRACLE CURES OF DR. AIRA

I

ONE DAY AT dawn, Dr. Aira found himself walking down a tree-lined street in a Buenos Aires neighborhood. He suffered from a type of somnambulism, and it wasn't all that unusual for him to wake up on unknown streets, which he actually knew quite well because all of them were the same. His life was that of a half-distracted, half-attentive walker (half absent, half present) who by means of such alternations created his own continuity, that is to say, his style, or in other words and to close the circle, his life; and so it would be until his life reached its end—when he died. As he was approaching fifty, that endpoint, coming sooner or later, could occur at any moment.

A beautiful Lebanese cedar along the verge of a pretentious little street lifted its proud rounded crown into the pinkish-gray air. He stopped to contemplate it, overwhelmed with admiration and affection. He addressed it *in pectore* with a short speech that combined eulogy, devotion (a request for protection), and, oddly enough, a few descriptive features; for he had noticed that after a time, devotion tended to become somewhat abstract and automatic. In this case, he noticed that the crown of the tree was both barren and leafy; the sky could be seen through it, yet it had foliage. Standing on his tiptoes to look more closely at the lower branches (he was very nearsighted), he saw that the leaves, which were like small, olive-green feathers, were partially coiled around each other, it was the end of fall, and the trees were struggling to survive.

"I honestly don't believe that humanity can continue much longer on this path. Our species has reached a point of such dominance on the planet that it no longer has to confront any serious threat, and it seems that all we can do is continue to live, enjoying what we can without having to risk anything. And we keep moving forward in that direction, securing what is already safe. With each advance, or retreat, no matter how gradual, irreversible thresholds are crossed, and who knows which we have already crossed or are crossing at this very moment. Thresholds that could make Nature react, if we understand by Nature, life's general regulatory mechanism. Maybe this frivolity we've achieved has irritated Her; maybe She cannot allow one species, not even our own, to be freed from its most basic needs ... Of course I am personalizing this quite perversely, reifying and externalizing forces that exist within us, but it doesn't matter because I understand myself."

Such things to say to a tree!

"It's not that I'm prophesying anything, especially not catastrophes and plagues, not even subtle ones, no way! If my reasoning is correct, the corrective mechanisms are at work within our present state of well-being and as a part of it ... I just don't know how."

He had started walking and was already at some distance from the tree. Every now and then he would stop again, and with a look of deep concentration he would stare at some random spot in his surroundings. These were abrupt stops, which lasted about half a minute and did not occur with any discernible regularity. He alone knew what they were in response to, and it was improbable that he would ever tell anybody. They were stops of embarrassment; they coincided with a memory, which emerged out of the folds of his idle digressions, of a blunder. It wasn't as if he enjoyed these memories, on the contrary; he simply could not prevent them from rising suddenly in his mental tide. And such an appearance was powerful enough to paralyze his legs, make him stand still, and he would have to wait for a fresh impetus to start walking again. Time lifted him out of the shame of the past ... It had already done so; it had already carried him into the present. Such blunders were cessations of time, where everything coagulated. They were mere memories, stored away in the most impregnable of safe boxes, one no stranger could open.

They were small, ridiculous, and perfectly private disgraces—a moment of awkwardness, a faux pas, which had affected nobody but himself; they had made strong impressions on him, clots of meaning that blocked the flow of events. For some reason, they were irreducible. They resisted translation, such as a transfer to the present. Whenever they appeared, they paralyzed him in the middle of his somnambulistic activities, which is what would bring them out of their labyrinthine lair of the past. The more he walked, the greater the chance that he would catch one, against his will. This turned his endless strolls into trajectories through the bifurcated maze of his youthful past. Perhaps, after all, there was some kind of regularity that drew a pattern through space-time, these cessations creating an empty distance ... But he would never be able to find a solution to his strange theorem if he couldn't explain why his steps stopped whenever a memory of this kind made its appearance; standing still and staring at one spot could be explained as an attempt to dissemble, perhaps pretend that this spot interested him so much that he had no choice but to stop. But the cessation in itself, the relationship between the blunder and paralysis, remained obscure, as long as he did not resort to psychological interpretations. Perhaps the key could be found in the very nature of those embarrassing moments, in their essence or common denominator. If that were the case, what was happening was a repetition compulsion in its most purely formal aspect.

Digging deeper into the issue, of course, was the fact that these blunders had occurred. They happen to everybody. They are the inevitable result of sociability, and the only solution is to forget. Truly, the only one, because time doesn't go backwards, so they cannot be fixed or erased. And because he could not depend on forgetting (he had the memory of an elephant), he had taken recourse in solitude, in almost complete isolation from his fellows, in this way guaranteeing at least the minimization of the effects of his incurable awkwardness, his bewilderment. And his somnambulism, which existed on a different level of his consciousness and his intentionality, should move in the same direction, like an a posteriori redemption, if in fact a somnambulist acted with the elegance of perfect efficiency.

To be honest with himself, he had to admit that blunders were not the only issue; the common denominator actually was spread along a rather sinuous path, which turned out to be not so easy to follow. Or perhaps one had to broaden the definition of a blunder: it could also include small infamies, acts of stinginess, accounting errors, cowardice; in other words, anything that feeds retrospective and private shame. And it was not as if he blamed himself (though during those stops a voice inside would shout: "What an idiot! What an idiot!"), for he had admitted they were inevitable at the moment they had occurred. At least he took comfort in their insignificance, for they had never been crimes, nor had there ever been any victims other than his own self-esteem.

In any case, he had promised himself they would never happen again. To achieve this he didn't need to do anything but remain alert and avoid precipitous behavior, always acting within the rules of honor and a proper upbringing. In his practice as a miracle healer, a blunder could have dire consequences.

In a novel, blunders are set up with great deliberation, with ingenuity and care, which is quite paradoxical, for it turns out to be more natural and spontaneous to write a scene in which everybody behaves properly. Dr. Aira equated every act that was morally, intellectually, or socially wrong with an act of violence, one that left a scar on the eminently smooth skin of his ideal behavior. He was one of those men who could not conceive of violence.

Although he knew this to be absurd, he could not help imagining that were he to find himself in a robbers' cave, for example, among the most brutal of criminals, he would be able to avoid violence if he behaved reasonably, talking and listening to others' opinions and expressing his own. Even if the situation was ripe for violence, even if the robbers had caught him spying ... But how could they have caught him if he himself had not planned his intrusion? And he had sworn he'd never again get himself into an awkward situation like that. It's true that he could have entered that hypothetical cave by mistake, thinking it was empty and unoccupied; that's where paying attention came into play—that he should always be awake, never blink. Which was easier said than done, though to achieve it, he had a practice, an ascesis, which he had made his life plan. Even so, a miraculous incident could occur in which he suddenly opened his eyes and found himself in a cave full of stolen goods, and before he had time to react a gang of suspicious-looking subjects entered ... Of course, he was smack in the middle of the realm of the imaginary, of remote possibilities. Once he was there with them, what would prevent him from establishing a civilized conversation with the robbers, getting them to understand what had happened, the teleporting, the somnambulism ... ? But in that case the robbers would also be part of the fiction, the theory, and his persuasive success would have no demonstrative value. Real reality was comprised of blood and blows and shouts and the slamming of doors. In the long run, the glaze of courtesy got scratched, if not from the causal line of facts then from another, inevitably, from the line that emerged out of the bifurcation of time.

An enormous dog lying at the entrance to an auto repair shop stood up when it saw him then bared its teeth. He instantaneously broke out in a cold sweat. What an incredible lack of consideration on the part of the owners of these animals, leaving them loose on the sidewalk and responding to any complaint with the familiar, "He's friendly, he won't do anything." They say it with total sincerity, and full conviction, but they haven't stopped to think that nobody else has any reason to share that conviction, much less so when facing a black mantle the size of a motorbike hurtling toward them ...

His first encounter with the world of paranormal medicine had been through dogs. When he was a child in the town of Coronel Pringles, Mayor Uthurralt issued an order mercilessly expelling all of them from the city limits, without exception or appeal. Fear alone (it was the era of the terrible polio epidemic) guaranteed compliance, this in spite of the usually strong attachment between pets and their owners. Moreover, the expulsion was temporary, though it ended up lasting three years, and nobody had to really get rid of their pets: all they had to do was find a place for them somewhere in the countryside. In a town that lived off rural activities, everybody had a friend or relative with a plot of land nearby, and that's where the dogs were sent. The problem was that the only veterinarian in Pringles was separated from his patients, and although he accepted having to travel to treat them (he had no choice if he wanted to keep working), the process was expensive and bothersome. And it made it difficult to neuter male puppies when they reached reproductive age, operations that had become that much more urgent under the present circumstances. Faced with the truly ghastly alternative of handing them over to farm hands, who could carry out the brutal procedure only with a branding iron and without any sterilization, some doled out a lot of money, others shut their eyes, most hesitated ... It was an opportunity for a local photographer, nicknamed the Madman, to start a business of long-distance, painless neutering, which became all the rage in Pringles during that period. Dr. Aira, at the time a child of eight, heard of this through rumors that had been grossly distorted in the echo chamber of his childhood circle. At that time, such subjects were rarely discussed, especially in a decent middle-class family; his little friends, all from poor families because he lived in a neighborhood of hovels, did not suffer from this disadvantage, but their families' amazing ignorance and credulity fully compensated for this lack.

The Madman's method was of exemplary absurdity, for it consisted of a fairly long series of penicillin shots given to the dogs' owners, shots that neutered the animal in absentia. At least that's what could be garnered from the stories that were making the rounds. He could never find out anything more, and perhaps there was nothing more. Nor did he ever learn in any reliable way if anyone had actually agreed to submit to this strange treatment. But this information was enough for him to reinvent on his own the possibility of action from a distance, of discontinuous efficiency, one that created a new continuum out of heterogeneous elements, and from then on his entire mental landscape was based on this premise. Soon thereafter the Madman's method ceased to be used (if it ever had been in reality), this in the wake of a scandal of vast proportions. A headless dog was born on a nearby farm, a cocker spaniel whose body stopped at his neck but who nevertheless survived and even grew to adulthood.

Inevitably, popular imagination connected one thing to the other, and the Madman, perhaps also frightened by the effects of his manipulations, threw in the towel, for the time being. Dr. Aira didn't know what ever happened to that dog; at some point it must have died, like any other dog. Many people in the town went to see it (it hadn't been sent away). Apparently, the animal was very lively: hyperactive as well as acephalous. Its nervous system ended in a bulb on top of its neck, and this protuberance, like a Rosetta stone, was covered with markings that represented eyes, nose, mouth, and ears, scribbles it made do with. Under other circumstances the fact that such a monster was viable would have attracted the attention of scientists all around the world; it should have been considered a kind of miracle. But country folks are accustomed to such miracles—paradoxically, they used to be more accustomed to them, back then when they lived in greater isolation, without radio or television or magazines; their entire world was the small world they lived in, and their laws made room for exceptions and extensions, as a totality always does.

If this had happened with a dog, why couldn't it happen with a man? This possibility, the infinite and infinitely fantastic possibility, established the always so immediate limitations of reason. All that polite reasoning he planned to use with the robbers in the cave showed itself to be just one form, a form contiguous with life's many violent insanities. Reason is one mode of action, nothing more, and it has no special privileges. The fact that he had extended its reach to cover everything, like a panacea he hoped would make up for the shortcomings of action, was simply a personal quirk, and a very symptomatic one: it showed his true colors and the error in which he lived. Because those eminently reasonable characters he so much admired and whom he modeled himself after (like Mariano Grondona), were considered reasonable only *pour la galerie*—that's how they made their living—but they also had a real life in which they were not reasonable, or they were only intermittently and carelessly so, depending on the circumstances, as these things should be. In order for action to be effective, one had to depart from the purely reasonable, which would always be an abstract way of thinking devoid of any truly practical use.

One could depart through realism. Realism was obviously a representation, but precisely for this reason it could become a spontaneous way of being when applied to an entire discourse. Realism was a deviation from the reasonable; a theory pointed to a path that was a straight line, but the realistic man who knew how to live followed one that was roundabout and had twists and turns ... each one of these detours away from the straight path was by nature and intention Evil. It didn't matter that it was an attenuated Evil, one without consequences; its essence was still Evil, and it had to be for the detour to be effective and for realism to be created, and for reality to be seen through realism, finally, real reality, so distinct from the pale fantasies of reason ... Perhaps there, in that eminently benevolent utility, resided Evil's purpose.

An ambulance siren broke through the quiet morning air of

the neighborhood, apparently in a great hurry but also apparently taking a quite roundabout route, coming and going through those small and empty streets as if it couldn't find its way. The physical phenomenon that makes a siren sound different when it is approaching from when it is departing, even when the distances are equal, is well known. That difference allowed Dr. Aira to reconstruct the intricate route the ambulance was taking. This is what he had been doing for the past few minutes without realizing it, absorbed as he was in other thoughts and memories; now, with the dog hurling itself at him, he became alarmed when he realized that the sound, with all its comings and goings, was drawing a circle that was closing in on him ... There it was again, that cursed ambulance, which had been pursuing him in dreams and throughout wakeful nights, in fantasy and reality, always driving with its siren blasting along the uncertain edge of two realms! Fortunately, it had never caught up with him. Like in a nightmare that is never consummated but for that very reason is even more nightmarish, at the very last minute, just when it was about to catch him, he would escape through the center of the labyrinth, though he never knew exactly how ... That was the moment of extreme danger, with terror ripping through the seams of reality, when he would transfer that sense of danger to some other element, as he had just now done with the dog, thereby establishing a continuum and crossing over that bridge, heading in the opposite direction of that fear ...

The siren's sudden escalation to ultrasound, combined with a screech of brakes just inches away, shook him out of his daydream. The scene plunged into a present where there was no room for thinking. That's why he needed a few seconds to realize that the ambulance had found him and that he didn't know what to do. The unthinkable had finally occurred. The dog, caught in the middle of its leap by harmonies only it could hear, did a somersault in the air, then began racing around in circles.

He turned, gathering up his scattered dissembling reflexes, and adopted a casual expression, one of almost indifferent curiosity. Two young doctors were getting out of the ambulance and starting to walk toward him (in any case, they were only a step away) with a decisive air, while the driver, an enormous black man in a nurse's uniform, got out of the side door and started walking around the vehicle. He froze, pale and with his mouth dry.

"Dr. Aira?" said one of the doctors, as if he were confirming rather than asking.

He nodded briefly. There was no point in denying it. He still couldn't believe that the ambulance, after such a long time, after so many twists and turns, had actually reached him. But there it was, materialized and white, so real as to be almost unbearable. And it had lifted him out (the doctor's words had proved it) of that urban anonymity where one watches ambulances drive by ...

"We've been looking for you for a long time; you can't imagine how hard you've made it for us."

"At your house," the other said, "they told us you had gone out for a walk, and we went out to find you ..."

The driver joined the group and interrupted, jokingly:

"No chance in hell we would have imagined you'd walk straight down this street!"

The others chuckled with complicity, eager to get to the

point; all three had spoken at once, and therein ended the introductory chat.

"I am Dr. Ferreyra, pleased to meet you," said one of the doctors, holding out his hand, which Dr. Aira took mechanically. "We have a desperate case, and they have requested your intervention."

"Come, let's continue our conversation in the 'living room' so we don't waste any more time."

And in a split second, and with worrying ease, they were inside the ambulance, the huge black man was behind the wheel, and they took off like lightning—the siren wailing, trees and houses slipping past like screen shots, all accompanied by the dog's furious barking ... Dr. Aira's attention collapsed with the excess. The two young doctors were talking constantly, taking turns or overlapping, their eyes flashing, their handsome, youthful faces bathed in an invisible sweat. He heard them (too well) but didn't register what they were saying, which didn't worry him at the moment as he was certain that they were simply reciting the script they'd memorized, which they would be able to repeat as many times as necessary; perhaps they were already repeating it. The first thing he asked himself, once he was able to think again, was why he had agreed to get into this vehicle. He justified it by saying that it had been the simplest thing to do, the one that created the fewest problems. Now all he had to do was get out and return home; they were not going to get too carried away with this masquerade, because then it would turn into a kidnapping, and they would get into trouble with the police. His only concern now (and it didn't present an insurmountable obstacle) was to refuse their requests and suggestions, refuse everything.

Whenever an unexpected incident disrupted his plans, he would become completely bewildered; as this happened to him fairly frequently, he had invented a remedy and had assembled a small recuperation kit, which he always carried in his pocket. The theory behind this solution was that he needed to restore the use of his senses, one by one, and the certainty that once he'd recovered his awareness of his senses, his ideas would fall into place on their own. The kit consisted of: an ampoule of French perfume, whose rubber top had a dipper immersed in the liquid, which he could remove and rub under his nostrils; a small silver bell the size of a thimble with a wooden handle; a little doll shaped like a bear, made of rabbit fur with a velvet cap he could rub his fingertips against; a quartz die with phosphorescent-colored dots, twenty-one of them, along with some other colors; and a piece of mint candy. It was so practical that he could make use of the entire kit in a few seconds. He carried it in a little tin box in his jacket pocket. But he had to use it secretly, which was impossible on this occasion, so he left it in his pocket. Moreover, he didn't need to recover any particular level of lucidity to do so, quite the contrary. He knew he had a tendency to think too much, and he could even fall into his own traps.

They were the ones setting the trap. All he had to do was get out of it. The trap consisted of making him think until he'd convinced himself that it wasn't a trap.

"Forgive me, I still haven't introduced myself," the other doctor said. "I am Dr. Bianchi."

They shook hands, without having to stretch out their arms because they were sitting so close to each other on the folding benches in the back of the ambulance.

This was his indication that they were willing to begin repeating the explanations, now with the advantage of pretending they were just filling in details that had been left unclear or ambiguous. And the fact was, in what followed Dr. Aira managed to catch the word "Piñero," which he had been expecting without realizing it. All the persecution he and his art were subjected to was instigated by the sinister Dr. Actyn, chief of medicine at Piñero Hospital. All the attacks and the ambushes came from there, and led to there, to the old hospital in the Lower Flores District of Buenos Aires.

Okay, so what was it about this time? And what was it going to be about? He knew it by heart: a terminal patient, the failure of conventional treatments, the family's anguish ... The thematic spectrum was so limited ... Always the same! All the old miseries, even more depressing when taken out of their framework of absolute truth, of all or nothing ... Because a doctor, as opposed to a patient, could always try again, even when it wasn't fictional, as it surely was here. The possibility that it was a lie contaminated the very truth it was based on: the plausible itself.

A small curtain divided the ambulance longitudinally. They pulled it back: there was the patient, strapped to the stretcher. So they'd brought him here! Those wretches stopped at nothing! "All's fair in war," Actyn must have thought.

The two doctors leaned over him with such intense, professional attention that they forgot about Dr. Aira; they checked his IV, his pupils, the blood pressure monitor, the electrical activity in his brain, the magnetic ventilator. The ambulance was

one of those new intensive care units. The patient was a man of
about forty-five who had evidently undergone radiation therapy
because the left side of his skull was bald, and the ear on that
side showed mutations. It almost seemed authentic ... But he
shouldn't think. He turned and looked out the window. They
were still driving straight down the same street where they'd
found him, still at very high speed and with the siren blasting,
racing through intersections like an arrow, one after another after another ... Where were they going? The houses, swept away
like exhalations in their wake, were all small and humble, a poor
neighborhood on the outskirts of the city. They seemed to be
accelerating constantly.

He started paying attention again because they were talking
to him. They drew a clinical profile of the utmost gravity. The
two doctors' self-assurance was astounding; they used techni-
cal vocabulary as if they had been brought up surrounded by
electronic circuits. All the machines were turned on, and they
illustrated the points they were making by pointing to a blink-
ing curve, a decimal number, an insulin intake chart. They had
everything divided into zones on an undulating tridimensional
grid that trembled on one of the screens like a multicolored cube
of gelatin; they focused in on the numbers, which they entered
into a wireless pocket keyboard.

"Are you familiar with this technology?" Ferreyra asked him
upon noticing his astonishment. "It operates with induced
evolving boards, made of dual proteins. Would you like to try?"
he asked, handing him the keyboard.

"No! I'm afraid of doing something foolish."

"You see, all these marvels of science cannot prevent ... "

Yeah, yeah, you can't get me to bite that. Where's the camera? It had undoubtedly been easy to hide among all those machines, and Actyn was probably watching him at that very moment, surrounded by his henchmen, recording everything. Now he understood why the ambulance kept driving in a straight line without turning down any side streets: turning interfered for a few instants with the transmission of the image, and Actyn didn't want to miss a single second; this worried Dr. Aira, for it indicated that all they needed from him was a momentary slip ...

What were they telling him? Had they reached the core of the issue?

" ... your gifts, Dr. Aira, though from our strictly rational point of view ... "

And the other, at the same time:

" ... everything possible is being done, technology helps use up all possibilities of action ... "

What this meant was that the deployment of incredible machines hastened the intervention of magical healers like himself, for conventional medical science could almost immediately reach its insurmountable limit. Which established a link between him and them, making more plausible their request for his intervention.

And what might that intervention be? To bring a goner back to life? Pull him back from the very brink of death. As if that were something out of the ordinary! Wasn't this what always happened? Didn't everybody in extremis get rescued? That was the normal mechanism of interaction between man and the world:

reality would search for one more idea, search desperately for it when all ideas had already been thought ... and it would find it in the nick of time.

Of course they were hoping to see the exotic and picturesque part of the operation, the grotesque magical ritual, the touch of the ridiculous that they would know how to draw attention to, the blunder they would publicize in the tabloids, the failure. And of course he would not give them that pleasure.

Because all of this was the same as a medical "hidden camera," the difference being that they could no longer catch him off guard; they had already tried so many times that all they could do was risk "hiding the hidden," hoping to slip it in between levels.

He watched them talk, his attention waxing and waning at irregular intervals, as a result of which the two enthusiastic and youthful—almost frenetic—faces he had so close to his began to seem unreal. And they were, he had no doubt about this, though only up to a certain point; because they did belong to two human beings of flesh and blood. The intensive use of hidden cameras in the last few years (in order to pull off all kinds of pranks, but also to catch corrupt officials, dishonest businessmen, tax evaders, and criminal infiltrators into the medical profession) required using up actors at a phenomenal rate, for they could never be employed a second time because of the risk of blowing their cover. They had to always be new, debutants; they couldn't have appeared on any screen ever before, not even as extras, because given the high degree of distrust that had infiltrated society, the least hint of recognition was enough to ruin the operation. And that same, constantly increasing distrust forced actors to be constantly getting better, more believable. It was astonishing that they didn't run out of them; of course, they didn't need to be professionals (with the new Labor Contract Law, they were not strictly required to be members of the union), but in cases where a lot was at stake, it must have required a difficult decision to place the success or failure of an operation in the hands of an amateur.

These two were really good; they not only handled the jargon perfectly but they even had the gestures, tics, bearing, and voices of doctors ... Perhaps they were doctors who were collaborating with Actyn out of conviction; in that case, they were new recruits, because Dr. Aira knew all the original fanatics. Actyn had the necessary prestige and charisma to keep acquiring new adherents to his cause, which he called the cause of Reason and Decency. But it was a fact that doctors were also human beings, subject to the vicissitudes of incurable diseases, and whoever got "burned" in front of Dr. Aira would then be unable to use his services, even if the case was desperate. Hence Actyn's only option was to seek active supporters among the ranks of the youngest doctors, those who would least consider their personal risk. This explained why these two were so young.

Of course there was also the possibility that this was a real case. A very remote possibility, one in a million, yet it persisted as a pure possibility, lost among all the possibilities. In a different era, before these cursed spy technologies had been perfected, it would have been the opposite: the possibility that this was a performance would have been so improbable that he wouldn't have even entertained the idea; in those days, whatever happened was inevitably considered real. But there was no point in lamenting the good old days, because historical circumstances formed a block: everything would have been different in days gone by; you wouldn't have been able to record a blunder in order to broadcast it *urbi et orbi*, but miracles were accepted as a matter of course, because the precise boundary between what was and was not a miracle had not yet been established.

If he could trust in the existence of true symmetry, he might be able to hope, now that this boundary had been clearly drawn, that the corresponding boundary—the one that divided blunders from what were not blunders—would begin to dissolve.

Because blunders were a tributary of spontaneity, and without it, they would vanish like an illusion. In this respect, Actyn might have gone too far, and he might now be entering the arena where all his efforts were automatically sterile. Ever since he had decided to turn all his firepower against Dr. Aira and his Miracle Cures, he had burned through stages, unable to stop because of the very dynamic of the war, in which he was the one who took every initiative. In reality, he had overcome the first stages— those of direct confrontation, libel, defamation, and ridicule— in the blink of an eye, condemned as they were to inefficiency. Actyn had understood that he could never achieve results in those terrains. The historical reconstruction of a failure was by its very nature impossible; he ran the risk of reconstituting a success. He then moved on (but this was his initial proposition, the only one that justified him) to attempts to produce the complete scenario, to pluck one out of nothingness ... He had no weapons besides those of performance, and he had been using them for years without respite. Dr. Aira, in the crosshairs, had gotten used to living as if he were crossing a minefield, in his case mined with the theatrical, which was constantly exploding. Fortunately they were invisible, intangible explosions, which enveloped him like air. Escaping from one trap didn't mean anything, because his enemy was so stubborn he would set another one; one performance sprung from another; he was living in an unreal world. He could never know where his pursuer would stop, and in reality he never stopped, and at nothing. Actyn, in his eyes, was like one of those comic-book supervillains, who never pursues anything less than world domination ... the only difference being that in this adventure it was Dr. Aira's mental world that was at stake.

But, according to the law of the circle, everything flowed into its opposite, and the lie moved in a great curve toward the truth, theater toward reality ... The authentic, the spontaneous, were on the reverse side of these transparencies.

Be that as it may, the ambulance kept driving, the dog kept barking like crazy at the wheels (the sound waves of the siren, which continued wailing, must have carried the ultrasound frequency of the television broadcast, which the animal perceived), and the two dimwits kept holding forth. Now their alternating discourses focused on the patient—his personal circumstances, his history. How had that poor devil ended up in the state he was in? In the usual way, one any doctor could discover on a daily basis in the majority of the population: an unnatural diet and the exacerbation of the passions. This was the deadly duo that caused more premature deaths than war. Dr. Aira was struck by this old-fashioned and solemn vocabulary, but he reflected that this anachronism was enough to suggest a second interpretation on the next level into which everything would be translated if he succumbed: the "deadly duo" would turn into the abuse of minors and the enthusiasm for televised soccer.

In any case, whatever they were saying served no purpose other than as visual backup for the dubbing they would add subsequently to the film. It might even have been planned in order to provoke from him certain responses that in the dubbed version would become replicas of other sentences; because the only voice they wouldn't dub over would be his, but they could radically change the meaning based on the context, which they did plan to change.

One concept was repeated more often than the others: "vegetative state." In fact, the organism had already passed into the realm of brainlessness, after which all that remained was to continue to exist, no longer act, only react to the environment; at this point it could absorb only the effect of the medicine, without any further possibility of assimilating it in order to transform its effects. Of course, the phrase could be erased from the tape, but if it was uttered in the ambulance it was in order to provoke a certain response. Actyn must have been aware of his conversations with trees (how did he find out, the rascal?) and was attacking on that flank.

He was reminded of an episode in an old gothic novel: a monk with apostatizing tendencies demanded a miracle in order to remain in the monastery, an impossible condition for he was sure there would be no miracle. His interlocutor told him that if it was necessary, God would produce a miracle to keep him in the fold, and he told him to suggest one. They were sitting in the monastery garden, at the foot of a majestic tree ... The monk, somewhat at random, said he wanted "this tree to dry up." Needless to say, the next morning the tree was desiccated (the monks, true infernal Actynes, used a lethal chemical). Dr. Aira, that impenitent flaneur, would have asked to "dry up all the trees in Buenos Aires," the entire forest of strange crisscrossing lines he got lost in on a daily basis. And the miracle could occur! Or directly did occur ... After all, they were at the end of autumn.

He startled.

"Hey!"

Where were they? Where were they taking him? Had they gone mad? Would desperation have led Actyn to seriously consider violence? José Bonifacio Street kept going, on and on, always in a straight line ... Everybody thought the streets of Buenos Aires actually continued beyond the city limits, into the countryside, there turning into the streets of faraway towns, then again continuing into the countryside ... Past the small windows, which he looked through out of the corner of his eye so as not to take his eyes off the two little doctors, he glimpsed an infinite expanse, which must have been the Pampa. If it was, something had happened, something far beyond a joke. Nothing could be more realistic or more normal than a straight line, but following it one could also move into the marvelous. He had a miniature vision inside his head: the ambulance driving through an infinite and empty desert, and the dog running alongside the wheel, barking ... Finally he spoke, interrupting some elaborate nonsensical explanation in mid sentence—and they stopped talking, because this is what they wanted: for him to talk.

"The answer is no."

"No what, doctor?"

"I'm not going to do anything for this man, or for anybody else. I never have and you know that very well."

"But your gift, Dr. Aira ... The Miracle Cures ... "

"No cures or curates, and no monks, either. I have no idea what you're talking about."

"What do you mean, you have no idea? So why are you famous? Why do all the terminal cases beg for you?"

"I don't know. I've never ... "

"Is it an invention of the media? Why did we spend half the morning looking for you, wasting time we could have spent performing brain surgery? You're not going to tell us we've been duped."

"I've got nothing to do with it. I want to get out."

They suddenly changed tactics. The screens all turned red and began to emit blood-curdling beeps (surely they had secretly pushed some button). They threw themselves over the stretcher, shouting:

"A systemic collapse! He's failing! There's nothing to be done!"

In spite of their pessimism, they worked like the devil, shouting at each other, even swearing, all in an attack of hysteria. They applied electric paddles to the poor man, who was turning blue, seizing, writhing. The odor of strange chemical substances made it impossible to breathe. At the same time, the huge nurse stepped on the gas, as if he'd also been infected, and shouted incoherent orders over the siren's loudspeakers. Even the dog was going nuts. In the midst of this indescribable chaos, Ferreyra turned to him and shouted:

"Dr. Aira, this is our last chance. Do something! Save a life!"

"No, no ... I have never ... "

"Do something! We're losing him!"

He was groping behind him for the door handle. He had decided to throw himself out the door, if necessary while still in motion. Again they changed tactics. Suddenly, all the screens went blank, and everybody calmed down, as if by magic.

"We'll take you home, don't worry. The patient has died."

"You're going to have to sign a form ... "

"No."

" ... to explain the use of the ambulance."

"I've got nothing to do with it."

"Okay, good-bye."

They had stopped. They opened the door. As he was getting out, the dead man said:

"Jackass."

He could have sworn it was Actyn's voice, which he'd only ever heard on television. He stepped onto the sidewalk and looked around. The dog had disappeared, and the ambulance had already taken off, accelerating loudly. It was only at that moment that he felt a wave of adrenaline washing over his insides. This lag, like jet lag, had rendered him ineffectual, for the chance to beat the hell out of those charlatans had already passed. The same thing always happened to him: his indignation, which was torturous, came afterwards when he was alone, when he couldn't fight with anybody but himself. Always the same concatenation between time and blunders. A civilized person like him couldn't lament not having engaged in a knock-down-drag-out, but there remained a question about whether he was a Real Man or a scurrying rat. He was two blocks away from his house. He looked at the trees, the large banana trees along José Bonifacio Street, and it occurred to him that they were machines designed to crush the world until the atoms were released. That's how he felt, and this was the natural effect of theater. Who said that lies lead to the truth, that fiction flows into reality? Theater's misfortune was this definitive and irreversible dissolution. That was also its gravity, above and beyond the iridescent lightness of fiction.

At least he'd come out of it unscathed. His morning adventure was over. Once again, Dr. Aira had escaped from the clutches of his relentless archenemy and could continue (but for how much longer?) his program of Miracle Cures.

II

THAT WINTER, FREED from the material necessities of life through a stroke of good fortune (he'd received a sum of money that had allowed him to take ten months off from his income-producing activities), Dr. Aira dedicated himself fully to the writing and publication of his works. His worry-free state could only be temporary because once the money ran out he would have to again find ways to get more; but for once in his life he wanted to give himself the chance to be fully absorbed in his intellectual work, like some kind of monk or wise man detached from the practical aspects of existence. If he didn't do it now, at fifty, he never would.

One effect of his age was that he had lately begun to appreciate in all its magnitude the responsibility incumbent upon him as a creator of symbolic material (and who isn't creating this, in one way or another, all the time?). Because this material was virtually eternal: it traveled through time and shaped future thoughts. And not only thoughts but also everything that would be born from them. The future itself, the block of the future, was nothing more than what was enclosed in and exemplified by these forms that emerged from the present.

Of course, the transformations the forms undergo during their voyage through time render their destinations fairly unpredictable. Work done in one field can end up exerting an influence on another, on any other, even the most distant and unrelated one. Hence, his efforts in the field of medicine could create, centuries later, new styles in fields as different from his own as astrophysics, sports, or fashion. But what importance does this have? The true cultivator of worlds sows his seeds in change itself, in the maelstrom. Be that as it may, the idea enveloped him in a daydream—innate to him, in fact—in which everything was transformed into everything else, through beautiful transitions like works of art.

Paradoxically, the opportunity that presented itself to him— because of the fact that it was an opportunity, particularly an opportunity to think, to elaborate his thoughts without stopping for practical considerations—brought with it an urgency for practical action, an urgency to make something. That's what it was all about, because the other, theory, is what he had been doing his whole life, without the tyranny of necessity loosening its grip even for the few months he needed to transform theory into tangible objects. He was in the position of a poet who had written ten thousand poems and now had to seriously consider publishing them.

Things. Tangible things that could be held in a hand, placed in a drawer. The world was always praising "young people who make things," and for good reason. Because ninety-nine percent of the value of things, of their intrinsic beauty, is derived from time. A comb is useful only for combing your hair (and not even this if you're bald), but a two-hundred-year-old comb is sold as a precious object in an antique store, and a two-thousand-year-old comb is exhibited in a museum and is priceless. That's why it's worthwhile to make things in one's youth, because these are the only things we have the possibility of seeing made more beautiful by the patina of time, if we live to an old age. Those we make later remain for future generations, and we miss out on them. Dr. Aira had missed the chance, and he bitterly lamented this fact. But to make things now, at fifty, might bring back some inkling of youth; perhaps it would place time on his side.

The first thing was to begin publishing his installments of the Miracle Cures. First of all, obviously, he had to write them ... But at the same time he didn't need to write them because throughout the last few years he had filled an unbelievable number of notebooks with elaborations on his ideas; he had written so much that to write any more, on the same subject, was utterly impossible, even if he'd wanted to. Or better said, it was possible, very possible; it was what he had been doing year after year, in the constant "changing of ideas" that were his ideas. Continuing to write or continuing to think, which were the same, was equivalent to continuing to transform his ideas. That had been happening to him from the beginning, ever since his first idea. He had no other choice if he wanted to progress, for the subject was always the same: Cure through Miracles. His lack of dogmatism combined with his absolute conviction gave his mental elaboration on the subject a plasticity that held it in perpetual flux, which gave him an immeasurable relative advantage over the other miracle healers; on the other hand, it had prevented him from ever concretizing anything.

A related problem, which he had worked on laboriously, was his principled refusal to use examples. The established discourse in the genre was based on the exposition of "cases," clinical cases, surprising cases, exceptional cases ... But since all cases were exceptional, even the most typical ones, any text written within that system was condemned to being merely a digression. It was assumed that one could end up with an exhaustive illustration of an idea through the strength of examples. But for the idea to have any value, other examples would have to be able to illustrate it, so how could one achieve anything exhaustive? Even worse, the method of using examples in itself imposed a hierarchy between the particular and the general, a situation that could not stand more wholly in opposition to the very essence of his system of cures.

In spite of this, he had to think of a form of exposition that would be attractive to the general public, and the tradition of using examples was too deeply rooted to avoid altogether. After mulling the issue over and over he had come up with a compromise solution: to put into effect a do-it-yourself-examples mechanism the reader would be in charge of. He would confine himself to one example, only one "case," with which he would open the first installment (or rather number zero) and to which all the arguments would refer, thereby inverting the malevolent order of the general and the particular.

This *passe-partout* example had given him many headaches. Not its invention, which was easy, perhaps too easy, but rather the conviction that he would need to employ it. In order to avoid that ease, he stuck with the first one that popped into his head, and in the long run he had to admit that he had done the right thing. It was not a case in the strict sense of the word but rather a little fable, inspired by a pair of stretchy woolen gloves that were sold as "magic gloves"; he had a pair, which he wore when he went on strolls in the winter; their "magic" consisted of both of them being exactly the same, so either could be worn on the right or the left hand indistinguishably. In turn, all the pairs of gloves were the same, all one size, and they fit all hands, from a little girl's to a truck driver's; their adaptability, just like their trick of bilateral symmetry, was due to the elasticity of their knit, and therein lay all the magic. What he imagined was the existence of a unique pair of truly "magic gloves," made out of thick red leather with angora fur lining—hence very thick—that would have the property of giving the hands that wore them (but only while they were wearing them) the sublime piano-playing virtuosity of an Arrau or an Argerich ... but they would be useless because one obviously cannot play the piano wearing gloves, and less so with such uncomfortable polar gloves. Hence, their miraculous charm would never coincide with any proof, and the underlying theory would be left untouched. Only by dint of useless miracles could one prevent a theory from degenerating into a dogma.

Choosing the "installment" format was a result of this kind of reasoning. He had come to it by retreating from more radical formats; for months he had played around with the idea of creating an album of collectible figurines, the figurines of the Miracle Cures, which would be sold in kiosks in sealed envelopes ... But the operational aspect created too many complications, and there were even some impracticalities on the conceptual side. So he rejected the idea of the album, as he had rejected many other possibilities that were as daring or more so. From these grand escalations of fantasies he would return to "degree zero": the book. And he would take off again from there, because the format of the book, with its classic simplicity that nobody respected more than he, limited him excessively. All that to-ing and fro-ing had converged at a point in the middle, which was the collectible installment, published weekly. The frequency would dictate his work rhythm, and the advantage of this over a book was that he would not have to finish the entire oeuvre before beginning to publish; that last part was the most important, because he had not considered a definite end to his labors; he saw it, instead, as an open oeuvre, which could incorporate into a fixed format the changes in his ideas, perspective, and even moods.

His fantasies of being an avant-garde editor turned out not to be futile, as many of the ideas arising from them were incorporated into the format he finally chose; and the "installment" plan was very hospitable to all of them, an additional reason to opt for it.

Illustrations were one of those features he wanted to incorporate. The idea came from some plans he had discarded, such as the figurines (and others), but it was also a natural for install-ments. When has anybody ever seen installments without illus-trations? Once he'd heard of a dictionary that had been published in installments, but besides this seeming too absurd to be true, a dictionary was ideal for illustrations, it carried them within, virtu-ally, for a dictionary is a systematic catalogue of examples.

Needless to say, he himself would make them. He would never even dream of asking an artist to collaborate, so great was his horror of relinquishing absolute control over any aspect of his work. He was reasonably skilled at drawing, which he practiced every day; however, they always turned out abstract. Only by ac-cident did his drawings ever represent anything. Nevertheless, he could, like anybody else, draw a comprehensible diagram, though he only did so when he was planning to fabricate some-thing. Recently he had filled a notebook with plans and models for fantasy garments, some in color.

These garments, which in reality had nothing to do with the Miracle Cures, as they were imaginative and highly elaborate items of clothing conjured up with the exuberance of fantasy, nevertheless constituted an important part of the project. In or-der to explain how he made them (because he had also had to invent this explanation, ex post facto), he had to start with the value of a text, any text, and by extension, of the one he might write about the Miracle Cures. Reflecting on the roots of value, he reached the conclusion that it was necessary to include an autobiographical component. This should never be missing, and not out of narcissism but rather because it was the only mecha-nism that would allow the writing to endure; and he wanted, oh, how he wanted! for his writing to withstand time, this also not out of intellectual narcissism but because with time his installments would take on the value of antiques, a value in and of itself, independent of the uncertain values of truth or intelligence or style.

As opposed to other objects, texts withstand time only when they are associated with an author whose actions in life—of which their texts are the only tangible testimony—excite the curiosity of posterity. Such posthumous curiosity is created by a biography full of small, strange, inexplicable maneuvers, colored in with a flash of inventiveness that is always in action, always in a state of "happening."

In any case, one day, out of the blue, while he was watching television, it occurred to him how delightful it would be to fabricate some garments, though more than garments they would be wire frames that would hold colorful fabrics—as well as wreaths, horns, halos, and bells—that he could wear at home to relax in or to energize himself or for any other purpose that might occur to him; the purpose didn't matter because the goal of this one-man theatrical wardrobe was to provide an interesting anecdote ... The purpose would formulate itself, and it would fit perfectly into his aesthetic-theoretical-autobiographical system and contribute to the creation of his personal mythology. It didn't matter what an enormous blunder this would be (even if in the privacy of his own family); at a certain point, he was willing to sacrifice himself for his work. Moreover, by taking this route he would reach a stage where the blunder, the fear of making a fool of himself, all of it, would be neutralized by being absorbed into the normalized and accepted figure of the Eccentric.

The fact that these garments, according to his idea of them, were a kind of architectural construction made of wire and fabric he would have to get into, meant he had to think up a way to equip them with a system of pleats that would allow him to sit down or walk around or even sit in the lotus position or dance. As a result, the drawings became more and more complex. Moreover, as they would be very large and bulky, and the apartment he lived in with his family was already crowded, he would have to plan for a second system of pleats that would allow him to store them in small stackable boxes, or ideally, in a folder.

The sketches he'd already made of these garments provided him with "ready-made" material he could use to illustrate the first installments; after that, he'd see. In any case, it wasn't worth worrying about at this stage. First he had to focus on the texts, and the illustrations would naturally ensue from them. For now, it was enough to know that he would make them, and this knowledge was enough to fill his expectations with vague figures.

As far as the text went, all he had to do was cull from his thousands of manuscript pages and begin to create the great collage. He could start anywhere; no introduction was necessary because the subject was already well defined in the collective imagination. Indeed, the charm of this material was like that of versions of a well-known story. Let's take one from the Bible, Dr. Aira said to himself, the one about Samson ... A funny story could have baldness as its central theme, which becomes a matter of state to the Philistines, and it would be funny because somehow or other everybody knows that Samson's strength resided in his hair. The same thing was happening here: life, death, illness—there's nobody who doesn't know what they're all about, which would allow him to create small, delightful variations that would seem like inventions even if they weren't (thereby sparing the author the exorbitant effort of inventing a new story).

Writing was something he couldn't do in a single block, all at once. He had to keep doing it, if at all possible, every day in order to establish a rhythm ... The rhythm of publication, so checkered due to the imponderables of the material aspects, could be regularized through the installment format, which also took care of the quantity of the product and its basic tone, that of "disclosure." These symbolic rhythms materialized when they were used as a framework for the rhythm at which things actually occurred. For in the meantime, life, both public and private, was continuing, and this *andante cantabile* system prevented real life from transpiring as a marginal event; through this rhythm it recovered not only the general flow but also each and every anecdotal detail, even the most heterogeneous ones. In this way he could be sure he wouldn't miss anything, nor would he fail to fully utilize anything. An episode like the one with the ambulance, which had left him very perturbed (so much so that it had been one of the triggers, along with his financial good fortune, for deciding to move into action), ceased to be merely one more "example" of Dr. Actyn's persecution of him, and became a particularity of the Universe of facts where there were no hierarchies or generalizations.

Given these characteristics of Dr. Aira's method, the publication would have to be encyclopedic. And although the word

"Encyclopedic" should never be written down, the open-ended and infinite totality of installments was nothing but a general and complete Encyclopedia. Therein lay the secret of the Cures, the secret he was aiming for, and therein lay the key to his entire enterprise: to give it maximum visibility.

Seen from this angle—as the penning of an Encyclopedia of all things from all times—the work revealed itself as the ascetic practice of a Superman ... There was so much to do! His life would have to last a thousand years ... One of the ideas he had discarded in the course of his fanciful planning was to adapt the format of false publicity brochures selling prepaid access to healers. A lifelong monthly fee would allow members to benefit from a Miracle Cure whenever they might need one. Like all the other projects he was enthusiastic about briefly then dropped as soon as cold reason snuffed out the flames of his fantasy, this one had not passed without leaving its mark. Everything fit into the text, which was made of marks, and not only human marks.

Basically, the discipline of writing consisted of limiting oneself to writing, to that work, with all its parsimony, its periodicity, its use of time. It was the only way to quell the anxiety that could otherwise overwhelm him, anxiety due to the immeasurable and self-propagating nature of the things that filled the world and continued to emerge each and every step of the way. There was a contrast, which could be defined as "curative," between the constant periodicity of writing, which was always a partial process, and the totality of the present and of eternity.

For many years it had been Dr. Aira's habit to write in cafés, of which, fortunately, there were many in the Flores neighborhood.

This unfortunate habit had combined with several practical imperatives until, during this period, he couldn't write a single line unless he was sitting at a table at one of those hospitable establishments. The viciousness with which Dr. Actyn carried out his campaign against him put to the test his will to continue to frequent them, for they were public places, accessible to him as well as to his enemies. But he had no choice if he wanted to keep writing. A dark cloud of paranoia began to accompany him during each one of his outings. At moments he felt observed, and with good reason. There were no direct assaults, nor did he expect them. But indirect ones could take many forms, and during these writing sessions on the Camino Real or on Miraflores or San José streets, anything could happen, or could be happening without him noticing, while one of his frequent raptures of inspiration was isolating him from his surroundings. He was certain that Actyn could recruit any type of human, any formulation of the human, for his operations of vigilance and provocation; hence it was not a question of recognizing his adversary by his looks ... He could not even say, just by looking, if somebody was observing him, because in a café it is easy to sit in a strategic position, avert the eyes, or stare at a reflection—dissemble in a thousand ways. He had developed at least one sure method for finding out if somebody was observing him: it consisted of yawning while secretly spying on the one he suspected; if he yawned in turn, it meant his eyes had been on him, because the contagious property of yawns is infallible. Of course, somebody who just happened to be looking at him at that moment might have yawned; and anyway, proof didn't do him much good, though at least he knew what to expect, which was enough for him.

Among the "practical imperatives" that forced him to go else-where to write was his wife's superstitious disdain for his intel-lectual activities, disdain that had been slowly turning into hor-ror ever since Dr. Actyn had mobilized the mass media in his campaign to destroy his prestige. More and more frequently she made a fuss, complaining that people recognized her, that they stared and pointed; she claimed that soon she would be too ashamed to leave her house ... She said it didn't bother him because he could always pick up and leave, as had so many other husbands who had gotten carried away. It didn't take much, not even an increase in hysteria. All a sweet young thing had to do was walk past him and he'd fall in love ... In fact, he wanted to love. His poor health no longer seemed like an obstacle. In fact, he wanted to love in sickness; suddenly this seemed to be the only true love.

Thinking about this, he asked himself a question: Why hadn't Dr. Actyn, who had tried his hand at so many options, ever con-sidered tempting him with a woman? He had set him so many traps that were so baroque, so elaborate, sometimes quite ab-surd ... but never the simplest and most classic. It couldn't be due to ethical qualms, because he had done much worse things. Was this not, then, the decisive proof of reality? How could he possibly have failed to take that into account? Did he have too much respect for him? Did he consider him above such tempta-tions? If so, how wrong he was! Because Dr. Aira's thirst for love made this the temptation he was most likely to succumb to. He was perfectly capable of falling into that trap, even if he knew it to be a trap, because he trusted in the power of love. Would it not have been the perfect romance, the valiant adventure that would make manifest all his fantasies in the material world? In fact, he thought that losing that battle would be the same as winning the war. But for some incomprehensible reason, Actyn had abstained from attacking him along that flank. Did he fear that the missile of love would end up piercing him? Or was he saving it for when all else had failed?

Without love, Dr. Aira was condemned to perpetual installments ... But he had to think positively and concentrate specifically on the practical aspects. With the arrival of the winter solstice, he felt he had reached the point of no return. He should already be making models of the installments, drawing the diagrams, choosing the typeface, the paper ... They would be installments, that was settled ... But in hardcover. He could be reasonable, but not to such an extent; some of his madness must survive. He had considered a thick, very stiff cardboard for the covers that would make a nice contrast with the small number of pages they would contain, though he still hadn't decided if there would be four or eight, but no more than that.

Nor had he figured out the costs. He would, needless to say, have to spend the minimum amount possible; in fact, he couldn't talk about "costs" because there would be nothing to offset them, that is, against which to measure them. The project didn't include selling the installments; to do that he would have to set up a company, register as a publisher, pay value-added tax, and a thousand other things he would never dream of doing. He would give them away; nobody could stop him from doing that.

The ideal thing would have been to operate with a dual monetary system, such as the one in Ancient China. There, they had official money for ordinary citizens and another for the poor, who were, of course, the vast majority of the population. The connection between the two, which never played out in reality, consisted of dividing the smallest unit of the official money—let's say, a cent—into ten thousand units; that multiple was the *sapek*, the basic unit in the poor people's system. A fistful of watermelon seeds cost a *sapek*. All business in the impoverished sectors was conducted with this money; the poor, the peasants, and children used no other, and these humble transactions met their survival needs. There was never any "exchange" because who would ever collect a million *sapeks* to exchange for one "cent" of the official money, a unit that had, on the other hand and on another level of life, a minute value, not even enough to pay for the cheapest item in a store, or the simplest dish in a restaurant? Whereas with much less money than that—under certain circumstances, a mere hundred *sapeks*!—a poor person could pay an entire month's food, shelter, and all other necessities. And everybody was happy and well fed.

III

EVEN FOR PEOPLE who lead a routine life without incident, for those who are sedentary and methodical, who have renounced adventure and planned their future, a colossal surprise is waiting in the wings, one that will take place when the moment arises and force them to start over again on a different basis. That surprise consists of the discovery that they are, in reality, one thing or another; in other words, that they embody one human type — for example, a Miser, or a Genius, or a Believer, or anything else — a type that until then they have only known through portrayals in books, portrayals they've never truly taken seriously, and in any case have never seriously considered applying to reality. This revelation is inevitable at a certain point in life, and the upheaval it creates (gaping mouth, wide eyes, stupor), the sensation of a personal End of the World, of "the thing I most feared is happening to me," is tailor-made to the frivolity of everything that preceded it.

There's no set age, as we know: everything depends on individual variables, which all variables are because the process of living is nothing but their accumulation. But it usually happens around fifty, which these days is the time when one begins to think that everything is over. In the subsequent psychic reshuffling, the horrified victim has an additional reason to feel bitter when he realizes that this discovery will no longer do him any good, that it is now a useless cruelty; if it had happened thirty or forty years before, he would have lived knowing it; he would have boarded the train of the real.

And this happens even when—especially when—the aforementioned subject has spent his life identified with the human type he later discovers he belongs to. In fact, in those cases the surprise turns out to be more disruptive and creates a deeper impression.

This is what had happened to Dr. Aira during this period. It would have happened to him anyway because the time had come, but the fact is that the revelation was unleashed by an incident that interrupted his publishing project before he had had a chance to begin it.

He received a call, which resulted in him attending a rather secret meeting in an elegant suite of offices in Puerto Madero ... and contrary to all his expectations he found himself embarked on the process of a Miracle Cure. Only a few days earlier he would have been able to swear that he'd never do it, that he was already past all temptation, that he had it beaten. His decision to publish installments had emerged precisely from his conviction that he'd left behind the call to practice. But, as we can see, man proposes and God disposes.

The people who contacted him were the brothers of an important businessman, the president of a petroleum holding company with vast influence on industry and finance, who had been unexpectedly stricken with a terminal illness. He was under sixty and of course didn't want to die, not yet. Nobody wants to. Human beings always cling to life, whatever the circumstances, and whether or not it is worth it. In the case of such a wealthy man, with so many possibilities of squeezing the most out of each day, the desire to prolong life burgeoned. The brothers tried, in their own way, to explain this to Dr. Aira, as if to justify themselves. Circumscribed by their professions and their education, they expressed it in their own terms: the holding company had embarked with great success on a process of privatization; it was one of a select group of local businesses that had managed to broaden its field of operations by reorganizing its assets. They were diversifying without losing strength and were on the verge of realizing the benefits of consolidation, the incorporation of Mercosur, the export stimulus, the retrofitting of their industrial plants with the latest technologies ... They got excited as they were describing it, even though it was obvious they were repeating a speech they had learned by heart, and it was no less obvious that they were reciting it to a total layman. A bit embarrassed, they returned to the subject at hand, suggesting that they were not singing their own praises but rather those of their sick brother, the brains and engine behind the group's entire operation, the natural head of the family. What they wanted to emphasize was the unacceptable injustice that he of all people would have to depart before seeing the fruits of his talents, his creativity in the business world, his boundless energy.

Dr. Aira's head was crackling, as if it were full of soda. He was also slightly embarrassed for having paid such close attention to the explanations, and he wanted to get back to the purpose of his being there. What was the illness? he asked. Cancer, regrettably. Cancer of everything. Large spreading masses, metastasis, the disease's uncontrollable growth. They pointed to a file on the glass desktop.

"All the paperwork is there, including his clinical history, up-to-date as of today. Though we suppose you don't work along those lines. It documents the failure of the best oncologists in the country and around the world. They no longer even bother to pretend to hold out any hope at all."

"How long do they give him?"

"Weeks. Days."

They had waited a long time to come to him. Anyway, it was impossible. They had probably begun alternative treatments months ago, and all available charlatans and healers must have already filed through. He felt paradoxically flattered to be the last one. They apologized with vague lies, unaware of how unnecessary it was to do so: their brother had undergone the conventional treatments with admirable stoicism; he had not given up even in the face of the most adverse outcomes ... Finally, he had given them permission to try the Miracle Cure, and, as he had done from the very beginning, he was bringing all his faith, all his trust into play: Dr. Aira could count on that.

There was nothing more to say. He looked at the file and shook his head as if to say: I don't need this; I know what awaits me. The truth was, he would have liked to take a peek, just out of curiosity, though he would not have understood anything because surely every entry was in medical jargon, which was inaccessible to him. Moreover, it was true that he didn't need it because his intervention occurred on a different level. The case had to be shut in order for him to come on stage; the clinical history had to have reached its end. And by all appearances, this is what had happened with this man.

The next step: he accepted the mission. Why? In spite of all his promises and precautions, he took the plunge. Once again, the well-known saying proved true: "Never say never." He vowed he would never do it (his interlocutors must not have known about this vow because they took his acceptance as a matter of course), and now he rushed to say yes, almost before they had finished making their proposal. This could be explained a priori by a defect in his personality, which had caused him many problems throughout his life: he didn't know how to say no. A basic insecurity, a lack of confidence in his own worth, prevented him from doing so. This became more pronounced and more plausible because the people who had requested his services on the basis of his capabilities and talents were, by definition, unfamiliar with his field, and little or poorly informed about his worth and his history. Hence, a refusal on his part would leave them

totally blank, thinking, "Who does this guy think he is, play-
ing hard to get like this? Why did we bother to call him?" It was
as if he could only refuse those who were fully informed about
his system, those who had already entered his system, and by
definition such people would never ask him for a Cure, or they
wouldn't ask him for one in earnest.

There was an additional motive, related to the previous one,
and the result of another defect, one that was quite common
but very pronounced in Dr. Aira: snobbery. This office with its
Picassos and its Persian carpets had impressed him, and the opportunity to enter into contact with such a first-rate celebrity
was irresistible. It's true that until that day he had never heard
of this man, and the family name was totally unfamiliar to him.
But that only magnified the effect. He knew there were very important people who maintained a "low profile" policy. And it had
to have been really low to go unnoticed by a snob of his caliber.
An unknown celebrity was as if on another—a higher—level.

But before all that, and as if obscured under a leaf storm of
circumstantial and psychological motives, his acceptance had
a much more concrete cause: it was the first time he had been
asked. Like so many other phenomena in our era dominated by
media fiction, his fame had preceded him. His own myth surrounded him, and the myth's mechanism had continually delayed
him from going into action, until there came a point when doing
so had become inconceivable. These wealthy barbarians had to
come along with their ignorance of the subtle mechanism of the
esoteric for the unthinkable to occur. In fact, Dr. Aira could have

gotten out of it by telling them that there had been a mistake, a misunderstanding; he was a theoretician, one could almost say a "writer," and the only thing that linked him to the Miracle Cures was a kind of metaphor ... At the same time, however, it was not a metaphor; it was real, and its truth resided in this reality. This would be his first and perhaps last chance to prove it.

They wanted to know when he could begin the procedure. They felt a certain urgency due to the very nature of the problem: there was no time to lose. They managed to include in their proposal a discreet query about the nature of his method, of which they obviously had not the slightest idea (this was obvious, above all, because nobody did).

Swept into the vortex of the blind impulse that had led him to accept the job, Dr. Aira said he needed a little time to prepare.

"Let's see ... Today is ... I don't know what day it is."

"Friday."

"Very good. I'll do it on Sunday night. The day after tomorrow. Does that work for you?"

"Of course. We are at your disposal." A pause. They looked quite intrigued. "And then what?"

"Then nothing. It is only one session. I figure it should last one hour, more or less."

They exchanged glances. They all decided at once not to ask any more questions. What for? One of them wrote the address down on a piece of paper, then they stood up—serious, circumspect.

"We'll expect you then."

"At ten."

"Perfect. Any instructions?"

"No. See you on Sunday."

They began to shake hands. As could be expected, they had left the question of compensation for this already marginal moment.

"Needless to say ... your fee ... "

Dr. Aira, categorical:

"I don't charge. Not a cent."

As awkward as his gestures, his facial expressions, and his tone of voice usually were, in this case, and only in this case, he had struck just the right note.

There couldn't possibly be a question of money, not for anybody there! And yet, that's all this was about. Money had been left out, but only because there was so much of it. In spite of this being the first time he'd ever dealt with such affluent people, Dr. Aira had responded with the almost instinctive confidence that only long habit can provide, as if he had done nothing his whole life but prepare himself for this moment. It must have been in his genes. In fact, someone as poor as he was couldn't charge people as rich as they were for his services. One simply places oneself in their hands, places the rest of one's life and one's children's lives in their hands. After all, billions of dollars were involved. As it was a question of life or death, it was as if the entire family fortune had been translated into wads of bills and stuffed into a briefcase. The amount was so colossal, and what he could charge, or want, or even dream of, was such a minuscule fraction of it, that the two quantities were almost incongruent. No matter how hard he tried not to think about the issue (he'd have time later, once he'd gone out the office door), he couldn't help making a quick calculation related to the installments. It was a calculation he made totally "in the air," in the pure relativity of fantasy, because he had still not asked for a single estimate from a printer; he had planned to do so in a few days, but this now prevented him, or better said, it gave him a good excuse to keep postponing it. Be that as it may, publishing was very cheap, and compared with the business they conducted here, the cost was marginal and insignificant. That's how he liked to think of it: as if the financial aspect could simply be canceled. This gave real meaning to his publishing business. He realized, in that momentary fantasy, that he could seriously consider things he had been placing in the "fantasy" category, like hard covers made of cardboard wrapped in paper with a satin finish, and full-color illustrations. The leap from the large to the small, from the fortune of these magnates to his trivial dealings with some neighborhood print shop, was so enormous that through it everything became possible: all luxuries, such as folding pages, vegetable inks, transparencies inserted between the pages, engravings ... And it's not as if he'd abstained from thinking about these options: one could almost say he had done nothing but. But he had done so as an impractical fantasy, even when he deigned to consider the most practical details. Now, suddenly, reality was intervening, and it was as if he should retrieve each and every dream, and every feature of every passage in every dream, and rethink them. He couldn't wait to be back in his house in Flores, open his file of notes on the installments, reread them one by one, because surely they would all appear marvelously new in the light of reality. He took a taxi so he could get there more quickly. For once he allowed himself the luxury of not responding to the taxi driver's crude attempts to engage him in conversation; he had too much to think about. Of course he still didn't have the money, and he had even rejected it outright. And what if these people, with the insensitivity so typical of millionaires, had taken him literally? It was highly probable, the most probable thing in the world. But it wouldn't do him any good to worry about it now.

That Sunday, at ten o'clock:
"Ding-a-ling-a-ling."
A housemaid in uniform opened the door. It was an enormous old palatial mansion in the Recoleta neighborhood. They ushered him into a sitting room to one side, where he found the brothers and a woman in a wheelchair, who was introduced as the mother. From the entryway, Dr. Aira had caught a glimpse of dimly lit rooms, elegantly furnished, the walls covered with paintings. This was the first time he'd entered such a distinguished house, and he would have loved to explore it to his heart's content, without rushing. But this was not the time. Or maybe it was? While he was exchanging banal greetings, he thought that in reality nobody was preventing him from doing just that, from wandering calmly through all those rooms. Because none of them knew what his method was; by definition they didn't know what to expect, such as him telling them that he needed everyone, including the servants, to leave the house so he could remain alone with the patient for one or two hours. They would think he was going to use some kind of invasive and potentially dangerous radiation; and they would be in a hurry to leave, dragging the old

woman out in her wheelchair; and all of them would climb into their Mercedes Benzes and wait at one of the brothers' houses. Why would they care, anyway? And he would have the house all to himself for that interval, as if he owned it; the possibility of slipping some valuable object into his pocket occurred to him, but he dismissed it as a too-sordid anticlimax.

Be that as it may, the interior of the house suggested an answer to an enigma that only now, upon intuiting its solution, he could formulate. What did his contemporaries do when he knew nothing about them? What did the great writers and artists whom he admired do during the often long periods of time when they were not presenting a book or making a movie or setting up an exhibit? Because of the amount of time he spent with books, he had grown accustomed to thinking of the great figures as dead, for the simple reason that for the most part they were: in order for their works or their fame to have reached him, some time had to have passed, and even more for him to have decided to study them; and this delay, more often than not, was more than enough for a human life to complete its cycle. That's why he would feel a little shock whenever he found out that this or that famous person was alive, simply living, without doing the things he was famous for doing. This created a kind of blank in which the nature of fame negated itself. He never understood because, truth be told, he'd never really stopped to think about it, but now he saw it all very clearly: what they did was live, though not just live, which would have been a platitude, but rather enjoy life, practice "the art of living" in houses like this one, or not as luxurious but in any case endowed with the comforts necessary to enjoy oneself and spend one's time without any concerns. Thanks to the link between reason and imagination, he felt at that moment that he could do the same from then on.

He had just sat down when he had to stand up again, because the other brothers had come in to tell him that the patient was awake and expecting him. They didn't sit down, so he didn't again, either. They told him that they'd given him his injections early so that he would be lucid at ten o'clock. They didn't know if it was necessary, but the patient himself had requested it.

"Perfect," said Dr. Aira, just to say something and without giving an explanation such as they must have been expecting.

In the blink of an eye, he didn't know exactly how, they were climbing the stairs to the bedroom. The moment of truth was approaching.

The truth was, he hadn't finished deciding what to do. He had spent the last two days considering his options with the same uncertainty he'd had for the last few decades, ever since that day in his far-distant youth when he had intuited the Cures. The idea had remained more or less intact since then, not counting the natural alternation between doubt and enthusiasm characteristic of a genuinely original concept. It had been the center of his life, the pivot around which his readings, meditations, and quite varied interests had turned. Of course, in order to keep it in this central position he had had to endow it with a plasticity that resisted any definition. It had always been right in front of his nose, like the proverbial carrot hanging in front of a donkey, indicating the direction of his prolonged flight forward. He owed his life to it, the life he had, after all, lived, and for this he was grateful. He could not complain about it just because it refused to give him a practical set of instructions at a decisive moment. He didn't want to seem ungrateful, like those infamous scroungers who spend twenty years taking money from a generous friend, and when finally the friend can't or doesn't want to do as they ask, they condemn him without appeal.

Moreover — as he had been repeating to himself throughout that atypical weekend — something would occur to him. It's not that he trusted his ability as an improviser; on the contrary, he had serious reasons to distrust it. But he knew that for better or for worse he'd manage, because one always does. It's enough for time to pass, and it inevitably will. It wasn't strictly a question of "improvising" but rather of finding in the teeming treasure of a lifetime of reflections the one gesture that would do the trick. It was less an improvisation than an instantaneous mnemonic. Evaluating the results was another issue. There would be time for that, too. After all, if it was a failure, it would be the first, and the last.

The door to the bedroom. They opened it; they motioned for him to go in. He entered ... And it was as if he had entered a different world, incomparably more vivid and more real, a world of pure and compressed action where there was no room for thought, and where, nevertheless, thought was destined to triumph in the end.

The first thing that struck him was the lighting, which was very white and very strong; it seemed excessive, though perhaps this was due to its contrast with the gloomy semidarkness in the rest of the house. Even so, it was the last thing one would expect in a sickroom, unless it was an operating room. He immediately turned to look at the bed and the man lying in it, which barely gave him a chance to register along the outer edges of his attention certain elements that contributed to the creation of a high-tech environment and explained the lighting.

The man in the bed warranted Dr. Aira's most intense interest. Never before had he seen someone so close to death. He was so close that he had already shed all his attributes and had become purely human. By the same token, this shedding had removed him from the human. His first impression was that it was too late. If there was even the remotest possibility of bringing him back to life, it would have to be via one of his qualities. And it looked as if he hadn't a single one left; perhaps, in the spiritual process of preparing himself for death, he had undergone a "cleansing" that had been set in motion by the illness. But this was not the case. Despite everything he and the cancer had done, one of his attributes remained: wealth. He may have cut all his ties to life, but he remained the owner of this house, and of his lands and factories. And that would suffice, for money had the marvelous property of including everything else. He should definitely start there.

Just thinking about it was enough to re-orient him in reality. He looked around. The room was large, and many people were there, all of them strangers, except for the patient's brothers. They were all looking at him, but as nobody showed any intention of introducing themselves, he merely greeted them with a nod and turned his attention to the room and the furnishings. There were chairs, armchairs, tables, bookshelves, and a lot of electronic equipment. It took him a moment to notice—even though they stood out more than anything else—two super-modern television cameras each on top of a tripod, one on either side of the bed and each with its respective cameraman: two young men wearing wireless earphones. The spotlights and large microphones with black felt heads placed at strategic spots apparently belonged to the same set-up, as did the echo-reducing panels and a technician sitting in front of a sound board next to the wall. He wondered, intrigued, if this was a custom he had never heard of, to record the final days of important people. That wasn't it, he found out right away, because one of the brothers, as if reading his mind, said:

"If you don't mind, we'd like to film you while you work," and without giving him time to respond, he rushed to explain. "It's to cover ourselves to the stockholders, just in case."

Dr. Aira mumbled something, and looking down at the ground, he noticed that there were no cables, which was quite fortunate because otherwise he would surely have tripped on them.

With a discreet signal from the brother who had just spoken, the two cameramen looked through their viewers and switched on the little red lights on their equipment. As if a lever in his body had been released, Dr. Aira stopped feeling natural. From that moment on, what was happening on the surface no longer coincided with the episodes of his psyche, which, now liberated from expressive restrictions, took on their own velocity. In a way, the exterior world could be deemed void: the nurses, the relatives who took their seats as if expecting to listen to a concert, and a small group of teenagers who looked at him with vague disapproval. What did he care! Relieved of naturalness, he felt as if anything was allowed.

He walked over to the bed. The man was lying on his back, his head and upper back propped against large pillows and with an orthopedic brace around his neck. His arms were stretched out on top of a sky-blue sheet, which was folded down over his heart. He was not wearing a watch. A thick gold wedding band was on the ring finger of his right hand.

His features were frozen into a somewhat ill-tempered, irritable grimace. He had not a single hair on his head. He was staring back at him, but his pupils were not moving. Dr. Aira tried to read those eyes that were locked on his, and the only thing that occurred to him was the melodramatic idea that they had the texture of death. Death is always nearby, and its shapes and colors inhabit all drawings of the world, in full view but also hidden, all too visible, acting like a narcotic on one's attention. One sees only what one wants to see. As if disappearance formed part of appearance. Sometimes one needs a word (the word "death") to make volumes and perspectives stand out. On this occasion the word had been spoken, and Dr. Aira understood that only through it did he have any chance of success. The only course of action was to take the man for dead, the activities of his life spent; not only could he consider it over, along with all the treatments and spiritual remedies, but he should, then begin from the other side. There was no other way to begin.

An idea was dawning on him, and its phases were cascading toward him. In reality, nobody was rushing him, but he had been thrust upon time. He wondered if he'd have enough space. When he turned his eyes away from the patient's, where they'd been glued, he felt as if he'd lost some of his strength. Even so, out of inertia, he kept figuring things out. To his right, on the wall facing the street, was a large French door covered with a thick, dark-red velvet curtain. He went over to it and pulled on the cord, which opened the panels sideways. There was a balcony. He didn't go out (he was afraid they'd think he was going to jump), but he glanced up. Right in front, between two tall build-ing, he could see a strip of star-studded sky. He returned to the bed, leaving the door open. In the room the cold night air began to be felt, but nobody objected. He looked back into the patient's eyes to recharge his batteries. He needed all his strength for what he was planning to attempt.

It was an old idea, which had remained latent in the depths of his mind all the years he had devoted to the Miracle Cures. He had never kept files with a strict chronology, and his papers had gotten mixed up again and again, a thousand times (his ideas were annotations on his ideas), so he couldn't be absolutely cer-tain, but he had the impression that it had been his first idea, the original Miracle Cure. In that case, and in accordance with the law of Decreasing Output, it was his best. It was based on the fol-lowing, if somewhat simplified, reasoning:

A miracle, in the event that one occurred, should mobilize all possible worlds, for there could not be a rupture in the chain of events in reality without the establishment of another chain, and with it a different totality. As long as the operation dealt with al-ternative worlds, however, it would be an impractical fantasy. As far as facts were concerned, there was only one world, and that was where the insurmountable veto against miracles arose. And the truth is, there were no miracles, as anybody with a little common sense could ascertain. Someone like Dr. Aira, who didn't even believe in God, could not entertain the least shadow of a doubt in that regard. Just because there had not yet been any miracles, however, didn't mean they couldn't happen; superstition, ignorance, gullibility all led one to think that miracles could happen just like that, naturally. On the other hand, it was possible to produce one, create one as an artifact, or better yet, as a work of art. For this, one only needed to introduce the dimension of human time, which was not difficult because time participated, by its very heft, in all human activities, and even more so in those activities that entailed almost superhuman efforts and difficulties. In practical, everyday terms, time is constantly producing a mutation of the world. After one minute, even a hundredth of a second, the world is already different, though not different in the catalogue of possible worlds but rather a different possible-real one, which is the same, because it has the same degree of reality. And "the same" is equivalent to "the only." It was within this transformational One, otherwise known as "the real," that Dr. Aira's idea for the production of miracles functioned.

Under these conditions, a miracle was simply impossible. But it could be created indirectly, through negation, by excluding from the world everything that was incongruent with it occurring. If one wanted a dog to fly, all one had to do was separate out each and every fact, without exception, that was incompatible with a flying dog. However, which facts were these? Here was the key to the whole thing: to make a correct and exhaustive selection. A wide field had to be covered: nothing less than the totality of the Universe. There were no pre-established or thematic or formal limits; the reach of the "compatible" was, precisely, total. The most far-flung fact or quality—or constellation of the two—could form part of the great figuration within which Miracles could or could not take place. Nor were levels a factor, for the line might run up and down (or to the sides) through all of them. The trick was to put into play the greatest of all Encyclopedias and to compile the relevant list from that. Who could do that? The customary response, the one that had been offered since oldest antiquity was: God. And to remain with that meant Miracles would have stayed within his jurisdiction. Dr. Aira's originality was in postulating that man could do it, too. It had occurred to him once while listening to the casual reflections of his friend Alfredo Prior, the painter. Speaking about paintings (perhaps Picasso's or Rembrandt's), Alfredito had said, "No masterpiece is completely perfect, there's always a slipup, an error, something sloppy." This might have been a factual observation, but it was also a profound truth that Dr. Aira treasured. Human acts not only contained imperfections but required them as the starting point in their search for efficacy. Discouragement in the matter of Miracles came from not recognizing this. If, on the other hand, this deficiency were accepted, creating a miracle would be as easy (and as difficult) as creating an artistic masterpiece. One simply had to give oneself time. God could revise the entire Encyclopedia and make all the right selections in an instant; man needed time (let's say, an hour), and he needed to allow himself a margin of error in the selections, trusting that they would not be critical errors. After all, that mechanism had an antecedent in the daily functioning of individuals: attention, which also compartmentalized the world, but which, in spite of frequent errors, achieved a level of efficacy necessary for its bearer to survive, and even prosper.

That's as far as the idea had come, and it was enough. The entire deduction of the reality of Miracles was there. Still pending was the elaboration of the historical aspect of the question (but this would be left for the installments), that is to say, why, in light of these discoveries, certain periods of history and modes of production were rife with miracles, and others had none.

Also left hanging, until now, was the practical aspect per se, that is, how to do it once it had been proven to be possible. When the theory is solid, the practice comes on its own. He simply had to dig in, and if he hadn't done so before now it was because he hadn't had the opportunity. Now the moment had arrived, and it was futile for him to reproach himself for having left the delicate question of the practice, in its entirety, to be improvised at the scene of events, especially considering the long stretches of free time he'd had over the years; because experience had taught him that practice couldn't be thought about like theory, or if it was, its nature changed, it became theory, and practice itself remained un-thought about. It was futile to have regrets, above all because he was already seeing the solution arrive on time for its appointment, and although it was very complicated, it appeared to him all at once, in an avalanche whose movement he knew well. Like a philosophical handyman, he carried ideas and fragments of ideas from other fields around in his head, and the way they instantaneously adapted to his needs elated him, as if all his problems had come to an end.

The operational tool came from the field of publishing. It was the "foldout" we've already mentioned, which had figured on his list of luxurious and unrealizable fantasies for his installments. Here the page foldout turned into the form of a foldout screen, with indefinite though not unlimited panels. Using the "foldout screen format" he could quickly and easily compartmentalize the Universe: thin and made of a very fine plastic film with wire stays, the screen could pass between two contiguous elements that were almost touching; flexible, it could make all the turns necessary; and its ability to continue to unfold made it possible to connect the most remote points as well as the closest one, and to divide up immense as well as tiny areas. All he had to do was pull the panels, this way and that, excluding areas of reality that were incompatible with the survival of this man. In other words: the Universe was now a single room, and the direct and indirect causes of his inevitable death were flocking indiscriminately toward the sickbed. All he had to do was raise the screen and stop them in their tracks. It was doable because these causes did not include everything that constituted reality, only a small part—well chosen, that's true—of the totality, which is why no sector could be excluded a priori. Once a "security zone" had been configured, the patient would rise from his bed, cured and happy, ready to live another thirty years. In the "open" world, such as it was now, he couldn't live; all the factors contributing to this impossibility had to remain on the other side of the screen. Or better said: not all, because that would be to fall once again into the divinity requirement; "all" that were humanly possible to find and isolate, those necessary to obtain the desired result, which, after all was said and done, was fairly modest: an individual cure.

He began to unfold the first screen without knowing where to put it ...

But I don't think I've explained myself well. I'll try again using other words. The work he was undertaking was nothing less than the identification of all the facts that made up the Universe, the so-called "real" ones in the narrow sense as well as in all the others: imaginary, virtual, possible; as well as groupings of facts, from the simplest pairs to the multitudes; and fragments of facts, that is, a thousand-year-old empire as well as one's first attempt to drink a beer. Facts had to be considered one by one; when they were grouped together it was to constitute another fact as particular as any one of its individual components and did not exclude the separate consideration of each of these; they were not grouped by genre or species or types or families or anything else. You could not take "a dog wagging his tail" but rather "this" dog wagging his tail at a specific hour and minute of a particular day, month, year, "this" particular instance of tail-wagging.

It was the complete Encyclopedia of everything, not only of the particular (the general was also included as a fact, made particular in order to appear on the list, on the same level as everything else). Nothing less than this would work. Because if the goal was to prevent from taking place an event that the entire order of the Universe threatened to make happen, he had to search through the farthest-flung folds of the Universe for every concomitant fact.

Granted, it would be impossible to compile such an Encyclopedia. This is a typical divine idea. But the originality of Dr. Aira's idea resided precisely in the passage to the human along the road of imperfection. He was not compiling it because he felt like it, or out of vanity, or emulation, but rather due to an urgent practical necessity: to produce an immediate and tangible result; and to do this, much less than perfection would suffice (at least: could suffice). It wasn't a question of giving the patient perfect health but rather of extricating him from his death trance.

Even so, it was a titanic task, for the listing of the facts was merely the qualifying round before carrying out the operation itself: the selection of the concomitant facts, those that have to be set aside in order to create a provisional new Universe in which "something else" could happen and not what was supposed to happen. By the way, these exclusions and the resulting formation of a field that would serve as a different universe had an antecedent: nothing less than the Novel itself. In fact, it could be said that to write a novel one must make a list of particulars, then draw a line that leaves only some of them "inside" and all the rest in an absent or virtual state. Which constitutes a kind of exclusion sui generis. There are many things a novel does not say, and this absence makes it possible for action to take place within its restricted universe. Hence, the novel is also an antecedent of Miracles, precisely because the events the novel recounts can happen as a result of what it excludes. Admittedly, here we are not talking about Reality but rather its Representation, but if the novel is good, if it is a work of art and not merely entertainment, it takes on the weight of reality as well. Then the cliché that states that a good novel is a true miracle becomes warranted.

We have divided up the work (first, the identification of all the facts, then the selection of the relevant ones) for the purpose of clarifying the explanation. In practice, it was all done at the same time. So that when Dr. Aira took off, he did so in a block, and his uncertainty included everything.

The foldout screen began to trace its white zigzag through the inextricable confusion of everything.

Yes ... Indeed ... The places it would have to pass through would appear on their own, almost without searching for them. To speak of a "search" was a contradiction in terms; as all places were being dealt with, it was enough to encounter them. In any case, what had to be sought were the paths that led through the overabundance of encounters. And within the action, which had already begun, within the miracle of the action, he was already dodging global cells, and in a matter of seconds he had become extremely busy. The elements came, magnetized by the capricious laws of attraction as well as the rigorous law of laws, and also by the lack or absence of any law. Hence, at the precise moment the screen was initiating its trajectory, the first elements appeared with clear outlines between which the lines of exclusion were drawn: those initial elements were none other than journeys and displacements: comings and goings in airplanes, taxis, shuttles, ships, subways, Ferris wheels, on foot, on skates ... Suddenly, Dr. Aira had a lot to do. The bar of exclusion in the form of panels of an elegant white foldout screen was already dividing up vast portions of the universe. Of all the airplane trips contained in the Universe, about half were left "outside," this to provide an acceptable margin of error; of course he couldn't know which were compatible or incompatible with this man's life, so he unfolded the screen in a zigzag, which anyway happened naturally, in order to increase the probabilities. If just one airplane trip belonging to the Universe in which the patient was dying of cancer remained "inside," everything would be ruined; but it was better not to think about that; defeatism was a poor counselor, and anyway defeatism, all defeatism, was also an element of the world that had to be sorted into the reconcilable and the irreconcilable; soon it would have its turn.

This first operation was already getting complicated. The screen's sinuous path was not one-dimensional, because along with the element "airplane trips," there also arose geographic places that connected these trips, and the various airplanes, the food they served on board, flight schedules, the faces of the stewardesses, the people sitting next to one another, the clouds, the reasons for having boarded the plane, and a thousand others; so the zigzag of the screen was magnified on various levels and in all directions like an enormous pom-pom. Dr. Aira attempted to draw the same zigzag along all its different routes while varying the proportions between the included and the excluded.

He did this because even though it was a question of humanity, and the theory considered the human as it was manifested in the real, he was fashioning a personalized cure. So he had to take into account—even if with broad brushstrokes and divinations—the man's lifestyle. Already he was operating in "lifestyle" and concomitant elements. He did not have a very clear idea (nobody does) of a millionaire's daily routine, but he could imagine it and complement his fantasies with common sense. For example, he needed only simple logic to determine that this subject must have traveled little or not at all by bus, in the world where he was dying of cancer as little as in the one he was in the process of creating, where he would be saved. But he knew he shouldn't rush to conclusions based on that fact, for his employees took buses, as did the friends and families of his employees, as did a waiter in a restaurant who had once served him, and the mother-in-law of that waiter, and people in general, all of whom became part of the system through its near and far-flung ramifications. Here the line of screens also turned into a pom-pom, and it was enough to think about the virtually infinite complications of the bus lines in Buenos Aires through any slice of time, any slice of the map, or through all the slices of all the moments since the invention of buses, to conceive of the number of turns the separator had to take. The screen cut through possibilities like sheet metal through a cube of butter, as if the material were made for it. Those who wanted to take the 86 bus to work tomorrow would have quite a surprise when they discovered that in the new universe the 86 didn't go down Rivadavia but rather Santa Fe, or that it didn't exist, or that it was called the 165! But no, nobody would be surprised because the "surprise" and every individual surprise, as well as every work routine (not to mention the names of the streets and the layout of the city map), were also objects to be sorted, and the resulting new universe, however it ended up, would necessarily be coherent. And, of course, public transportation in Buenos Aires would not be the only thing affected, far from it.

After journeys, it was time for light, an element that included everything from photons to chiaroscuros depicting the volume of an object in a seventeenth-century copper engraving ... It was a broad heading because there has not been a single occasion not swathed in light—for example each one of the journeys previously processed had lighting, and a whole series of lighting possibilities existed for each one, as there did for every conceivable or manifest occasion. In fact, this "generalization" characterized every heading; also the journeys or displacements, because could there possibly be an occasion that didn't imply, somehow or other, some displacement? So, everything was a journey, just as everything was light ... The screens' trajectories doubled back upon themselves to make it possible to update a previous trajectory and allow it to serve a new function.

Light presented an additional difficulty, because light, or rather lighting, occurs at a determined intensity, which is the manifestation of a continuum of intensities that can only be arbitrarily calibrated. But was this a difficulty specific to the element "light," or was it an attribute of all headings? Still within the heading already discussed, of journeys, there was also a continuum: the extension of the trajectory traveled. Or many continuums: of velocity, of the pleasure or displeasure with which the trip was made, the sum of the perceptions experienced en route ... And just as in the case of light, intensity was not the only continuum in play, for there was also the temperature, atmospheric resistance, color ...

Things were happening in less time than it would take to explain them. If Dr. Aira could have stopped to think he would have asked himself about the sequence "journeys-light." Why had he started with the first? Why had he continued with the second? What kind of catalogue was he consulting? Where did the directory come from? From nowhere: there was no catalogue, no order. The entire operation of the Cure had the perfect coherence of the plausible, like a novel (again). It wasn't like in the theater, where anything can happen, even something completely disconnected from all the rest; in that case, one could resort to a list of themes and proceed to remove each one using aesthetic criteria; in any case, if we wish to hold on to the theater metaphor, we would have to think about bourgeois theater, full of weighty psychosocial assumptions pretending to be plausible.

The plausible in its pure state, which was at work here, was characterized by simultaneity. Therefore, saying that after light came flags is just a figure of speech. The flags of all the nations of the world, those that had once flown and the possible ones that had accompanied them during their passage through History, with their colors and symbols, their silks or paper or retinal impressions, were underpinned by light and journeys. A luxuriant pom-pom of foldout screens cut through the entire sphere of the Universe, leaving some flags in and others out. Immediately, it turned to the cutting of hair. Screens. Hundreds of millions of barber shops, hairdressers, and scissors were excluded from the Cure's New World, while others remained inside.

Collaborating with this simultaneity was the fact that throughout the process the screens that were doing the sorting continued along their trajectory a little farther (there were no established boundaries), and a bit at random, tracing lines of division through other, contiguous categories, on other planes and levels. Dr. Aira accepted these random contributions because he was in no position to reject any help he could get. By the same token, he began to notice that the same screen could function as more than one partition through the effect of the overlapping of fields of meaning.

He was moderately concerned about the fact that every "heading" coincided with a word. He was not unaware that the Universe cannot be divided into words, even less so those of one language. He was also using phrases ("the cutting of hair" was one example), and in general he tried to turn a deaf ear to words, to inhabit a space beyond them. But words constituted a good point of departure because of their connotations and associations, their so-called "like ideas." Thus with the word "sex." He traced a crazy zigzag with the screen, leaving outside half of all sexual activity, past and future. The bundles of panels that rose and fell according to the participant, the pleasure, the modality, et cetera, again formed the familiar pom-pom. This was particularly delicate material, so he divided it up with particular brutality. The patient might get out of bed only to discover that he had not had a particular lover, or that he liked boys, or that he had once slept with a Chinese woman, but it was all worth it, if the tradeoff was life. That the same thing would happen to the rest of the planet's inhabitants, including the animals, was less important, because individual memories, which could only function with the parts that remained within the new universe, wouldn't remember anything. Many beautiful love stories would vanish into the ether, or would never have been.

The ends of the screen continued to exceed the fields of meaning and create others that immediately, and almost through the impetus of their unfolding, cut huge and savage zigzags. Astronomy. The ability of parrots and blackbirds to speak. The diesel engine. The Assyrians. Coffee. Clouds. Screens, screens, and more screens. They were proliferating everywhere, and he had to pay close attention to make sure that no sector failed to be sorted. Fortunately, Dr. Aira had no time to notice the stress he was experiencing. Attention was key, and perhaps no man had ever brought as much of it to bear as he did for that hour. If the circumstances had been less serious, if he had been able to adopt a more frivolous perspective, he could have said that the entire procedure was an incomparable creator of attention, the most exhaustive ever conceived to exercise this noble mental faculty. And it did not require an extraordinary person; a common man could do it (and Dr. Aira would have been quite satisfied to become a common man), for the Cure created all the attention it demanded. It wasn't like those video games, which are always trying to trick it or avoid it or get one step ahead of it; to continue with this simile, it should be said that the operator of the Cure was his own video game, his own screen, and his own decoys, and that far from defying attention, they nurtured it. Despite all this, the effort was superhuman, and it was yet to be seen if Dr. Aira could hold out till the end.

His depletion was physical as well as mental. For although the screens were only imaginary, the effort needed to unfold them and stretch them across the vast teeming terrains of the Universe was very real. He held them along their upper edges between the index finger and thumb of both hands, and he opened them by stretching his arms out wide, and since he could never quite reach, he had to move around, taking little leaps from side to side ... then he would return to touch up the line, expand or contract the angles. In general he avoided straight lines, which were drawn when he stretched the screens out too fully, because the straight line was too categorical and the selection had to be more nuanced: a fact could be included or excluded at the beginning or end of a folded panel—a singularity, which, however small, could turn out to be crucial; anything could be.

And there were screens that extended upward, or downward ... To stretch them out he had to stand on his tiptoes, or jump on a chair; if it descended, he threw himself on the floor or scrambled under the bed, under the edge of the rug—as if he were trying to bore a hole through the floor. He retreated and advanced as he stretched the screen overhead, all the while adjusting the angle or the direction of another one under him with the tip of his toe. As he could see nothing besides his screens, and the jungle of iridescent elements they were cleaving through, his movement around the room always ended with him banging into the walls, the furniture ... He stumbled frequently, and he was down on the floor more than he was standing up. Depending on how much impetus he had, he was either stretched out or rolling around doing spectacular half somersaults; but he took advantage of these involuntary plunges to hang the screens in places he couldn't have reached otherwise. Everything was useful.

He never stopped moving. He was bathed in sweat; it was streaming through his hair, and his clothes were stuck to his skin. He went back and forth, up and down, every cell in his body shaking, arms and legs stretching and contracting like rubber bands, and he was leaping around like an insect. His face, usually so inexpressive, churned like ocean waves during a storm, never pausing at any one expression; his lips formed all kinds of fleeting words, drowned out by the panting, and when they opened, his tongue appeared, twisting like an epileptic snake. If it had been possible to follow, with a stopwatch, the rising and falling of his eyebrows, one could have read millions of overlapping surprises. His gaze was fixed on his visions.

From the outside, and without knowing what any of it was about, the practice of the Cure looked like a dance without music or rhythm, a kind of gymnastic dance, which might appear to be designed to shape a nonexistent specimen of the human. Admittedly, it was pretty demented. He looked like Don Quixote attacking his invisible enemies, except his sword was the bundle of metaphysical foldout screens and his opponent was the Universe.

Thud! He crashed into a chair and fell headfirst to the floor, both his legs shaking; the crown of his head left a round damp mark on the rug; but even down there he kept working: his right hand was tracing a large semicircle, placing a screen that divided up the joys and sorrows of Muslims; his left was pulling a little on another screen that had excluded too many apples ... Now he was on his feet again, lifting the white accordion of a vertical screen that was crossing levels of reality as it sorted through "latenesses" and "earlynesses" ... ! And what looked like a tap dance meant to recover his balance was him hanging two screens that would exclude certain rickshaws and particular conversations. With his chest, his rear end, his knees, his shoulders, and head-butts, he corrected the positions, angles, and inclinations of the panels, enacting a true St. Vitus dance in the process. And to think that this grotesque puppet was creating a New Universe!

And so it went. One might have thought that the space of representation at his disposal was going to get overcrowded, that it was going to start to get difficult to keep inserting more screens. But this didn't happen because the space wasn't exactly the one of the representation but rather of reality itself. In this way, miniaturization led to its own amplification. Like in an individual big bang, space was being created, not getting filled, through the process, hence within each pom-pom an entire Universe was being formed.

In honor of reality, he had left the door to the balcony open. Through it long strips of screens were swept out into the heavens. He couldn't even see what some of them were excluding, but he trusted that in any case they would leave at least one particularity in each arena on this side. As often happens with difficult jobs, a point came when the only thing that mattered was to finish. He almost lost interest in the results, because the result that included all the others was to finish what he had started. He had really had to dig in to find out how demanding the problem of Everything was, what brain-racking pressure it created ... Only by living it could he find out; all prior calculations or fantasies fell short. Even though he didn't have the time, he fervently longed to return to human mode, which was so much more relaxing because it gives license to do anything. Nevertheless, what he was doing was deeply human, and given the mechanism of automatic re-absorption the Cure enacted, his exhaustion approached rest; pressure, relaxation.

In fact, the hinges on the last panels of each screen began to get welded to the other screens whose last panels were nearby, and with this the process of exclusion and inclusion was concluding. These welds happened on their own, one after the other, in cascades of billions that burst the heart of a second, of the final seconds. This produced a greasy white spark in the black depth of the Night. It was something like a nightmare, that "schluik..." Dr. Aira's utter exhaustion also contributed to this sense of feverish delirium, for at the very end of his strength he felt nauseated, as if he were suffocating; his ears were ringing, and there were red spots in front of his eyes.

But the important thing was that the siege had been laid, and the new Universe had been formed, as unfathomably complex as the old Universe had been until then, but different, and just right for the cancer of that man in that bed to never have been ... The work of the Cure had been completed right in front of his own eyes, half-closed from fatigue; his arms fell to his sides, flaccid, his legs were barely able to hold him up; the room, which he was now seeing again, was waltzing before his dizzy eyes; and in it the patient's bed, the spotlights, the cameramen, the nurses, the relatives ... The next time, he told himself in a state of exhaustion that rendered him idiotic, he would have to think up a machine that could spread out the screens for him. Compared with an automated system, more appropriate for the times in which he lived, the dance to which he had surrendered would seem like some kind of imperfect, handmade prehistoric Cure. But before thinking about an improbable second time, he had to wait for the results of this one.

It was a wait truly laden with unknowns. Already, when he witnessed the welds, and in the sudden passivity these allowed him after such dense, nonstop action, he perceived that with each "closure" the plausible had changed, only to change again with the next one; the closures, of course, didn't just happen; they were cumulative until they had formed one definitive closure. It was an extreme case of "doing something with words." The transposition of plausibles was vertiginous, and Dr. Aira had no way of knowing where things would stand in the end. That's what mattered, when all was said and done.

It didn't take long for him to find out. In fact, in the overdetermination of the present, waking up was accompanied by guffaws ... which was part of the nightmare, but on another level. Laughter was increasing around him, reordering and giving substance to the space of the bedroom, and from there to the house, the neighborhood, Buenos Aires, the world. He was the last to sort himself out and to understand what was happening; he knew himself and was resigned to such delays. In the meantime, the only thing he knew was that from that moment on whatever happened in reality depended on the angle some panel of the screen was hung, no matter how far-flung it was; for example, the one that had excluded from this new Universe of reality a bonfire, or the flying sparks of a bonfire, in the prehistory of the Maori people ... Amid the laughter, his eyes opened onto a New World, really truly new.

And in this new world, those present were laughing heartily; the cameramen were turning off their cameras and lowering them, revealing themselves as the two fake doctors from the ambulance on Bonifacio Street; and the patient, choking on his laughter, was sitting up in bed and pointing a finger at him, unable to speak because he was laughing so hard ... It was Actyn! That wretch ... Everything had been staged by him! Or at least that's what he thought. The truth is that he wasn't dying, he didn't have cancer nor had he ever, and he wasn't a very wealthy businessman ... The plausible had completely changed. Laughter was justified; happiness needed no other motive. After years of trying in vain, Actyn had managed to get Dr. Aira to commit the biggest blunder of his career, the definitive one ... And in reality it was: the blunder as the transformation of the plausible, that is, as a visible trace—the only one that could remain inscribed on memory—of the transformation of one Universe into another, and hence of the secret power of the Miracle Cure.

PRINGLES, 6 SEPTEMBER 1996

PRAISE FOR CÉSAR AIRA

"Aira is one of the most provocative and idiosyncratic novelists working in Spanish today, and should not be missed."
– *The New York Times Book Review*

"Aira is a master at pivoting between the mundane and the metaphysical."
– *The Millions*

"An improvisatory wildness that opens up possibilities where there had seemed to be brick walls."
– *The Paris Review*

AN EPISODE IN THE LIFE OF A LANDSCAPE PAINTER

"César Aira's strange and arresting novel, in the tradition of Jorge Luis Borges and W. G. Sebald . . . a memorable performance whose tone and oddly compelling vision are distinctly Aira's own."
– *Los Angeles Times*

"Aira's most dazzling novel to be published in English thus far."
– *The New York Review of Books*

"Astonishing ... a supercharged Céline, writing with a Star Wars laser sword, turning Don Quixote into Picasso."
– *Harper's*

"Multifaceted and transporting ... I get so absorbed that upon finishing I don't remember anything, like a complex cinematic dream that dissipates upon awakening."
– Patti Smith

GHOSTS

"An incitement to the sensuality of thought, of wonder, of questioning, of anticipation."
– *The Los Angeles Times*

"Exhilarating. Cesar Aira is the Duchamp of Latin American literature. *Ghosts* is an exercise in queasiness, a heady, vertigo-inducing fantasia."
– *The New York Times Book Review*

"Between hauntings, *Ghosts* is filled with Aira's beautifully precise observation of the texture of everyday life."
– *The Millions*

"Aira conjures a languorous, surreal atmosphere of baking heat and quietly menacing shadows that puts one in mind of a painting by de Chirico."
– *The New Yorker*

HOW I BECAME A NUN

"Oblique and darkly humorous. Through the marginal, Aira imaginatively explores the foibles of the human condition."
– *The Harvard Review*

"Aira is a man of multiple, slipping masks, and *How I Became a Nun* is the work of an uncompromising literary trickster."
– *Time Out*

"A foreboding fable of life and art."
– *Publishers Weekly*

THE LITERARY CONFERENCE

"Aira's novels are eccentric clones of reality, where the lights are brighter, the picture is sharper and everything happens at the speed of thought."
– *The Millions*

"Disarming … amusing."
– *The New Yorker*

"César Aira's tale of mad scientists, literary doubles and world domination offers a gloriously absurdist example of the 'constant flight forward' that powers his inimitable fiction."
– *The National*

THE SEAMSTRESS AND THE WIND

"Genius."
– Ploughshares

"A beautiful, strange fable … alternating between frivolity, insight, and horror."
– Quarterly Conversation

VARAMO

"Aira seems fascinated by the idea of storytelling as invention, invention as improvisation and improvisation as transgression, as *getting away with something*."
– The New York Times Book Review

"A lampoon of our need for narrative. No one these days does metafiction like Aira."
– The Paris Review